THE TEACHER FROM OUTER SPACE

by Justine Korman
illustrated by Bonnie Matthews

Troll Associates

Library of Congress Cataloging-in-Publication Data

Korman, Justine.
    The teacher from outer space / by Justine H. Korman; illustrated
by Bonnie J. Matthews.
        p.   cm.
    Summary: A student makes an astonishing discovery about the true
nature of his substitute teacher, who does not seem familiar with
the school routine and has his own way of doing things.
        ISBN 0-8167-3180-2 (lib. bdg.)   ISBN 0-8167-3181-0 (pbk.)
        [1. Teachers—Fiction.   2. Extraterrestrial beings—Fiction.]
    I. Matthews, Bonnie J., 1963-   ill.   II. Title.
    PZ7.K83692Td   1994
    [E]—dc20   93-24846

Printed in the United States of America.

10 9 8 7 6 5 4

Let me start by saying that I'm not one of those kids who likes school. In fact, I guess you could say I hate school. And the thing I hate most of all is having to talk in front of the whole class.

So of course I was dreading the day I had to present my science project. I think Mrs. Barney knows how much I hate talking in front of everyone. I worried about it in the bus.

Then a miracle occurred. Mrs. Barney didn't
come to school the day I was supposed to talk
about my science project. That meant I wouldn't
have to get up in front of everyone!

That also meant we had a substitute teacher.
He was pretty scary-looking. He was kind of
small and he walked funny. He looked like he
was wearing stilts.

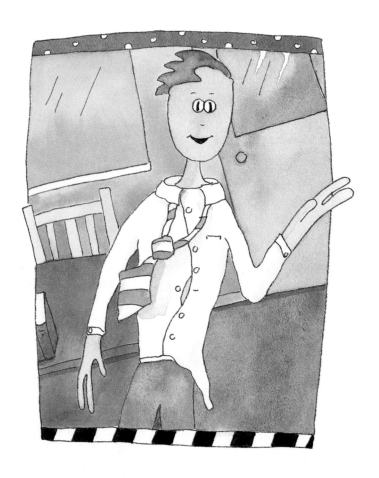

Goody-goody Gail asked the teacher his name. He looked kind of nervous. Finally he said, "My name is Mr...um...Mr. Ed."

Mr. Ed looked at the stuff on Mrs. Barney's desk. He stared at a pencil as if he'd never seen one before. And then he ate it!

I don't mean he just chewed on it, the way I do when I'm nervous. He ate the whole thing!

Nobody knew what to do with our strange sub. Then Gail raised her hand and said, "Mrs. Barney usually starts the day with our readers."

My stomach flipped over and over. I hated reading aloud!

Then another miracle happened. Mr. Ed didn't pass out the books. Instead, he used them to build a tower.

We all joined in. It was a lot of fun!

Of course Gail had to spoil everything. She told Mr. Ed we were supposed to read the books, not build with them.

She took out a book and started reading.

I took out my comic book. I was up to a really
exciting part, where aliens take over the earth.
    Suddenly a hand fell on my shoulder.
I jumped!

Mr. Ed jumped, too. Then he took my comic book.

Mrs. Barney gets pretty mad when she catches me looking at comic books during class. But Mr. Ed just looked through the book and smiled.

Next it was time for art class.

Mr. Ed didn't listen to anything the art teacher said. He just started painting. Pretty soon he had painted himself from head to toe!

The art teacher didn't know what to do with Mr. Ed.

"You certainly have an…interesting style," she said.

Mr. Ed didn't say anything. He just painted her nose blue.

At lunch time, Mr. Ed watched me take a tray. He got on line behind me. He took ten of everything.

Mr. Ed's lunch bill was over $100. He didn't pay it, though. He just gave the lunch lady some napkins instead.

Then Mr. Ed put all the food in little bags. I've heard of taking food home from a restaurant. But why would anyone want food from the school cafeteria?

During recess, Mr. Ed played with us instead of sitting inside with the other teachers. We all had a great time.

When the bell rang, Mr. Ed just kept playing. We all had to drag him back to class.

After recess Mr. Ed asked us to tell him something about ourselves. He told me to go first.

I didn't even have time to get nervous. I told everyone about my comic book collection. And nobody laughed at me! In fact, they all thought it was pretty neat! I couldn't believe I talked in front of the whole class—and it was fun!

For the first time in my life, I was actually sorry when the bell rang at the end of the day. I think everyone felt sad saying good-bye to Mr. Ed.

I walked slowly to the bus that day. I was wishing that Mr. Ed could always be our teacher.

Then I remembered that Mr. Ed still had my comic book. I raced back to the classroom.

When I got to the doorway, Mr. Ed was sitting at Mrs. Barney's desk. He didn't see me.

Mr. Ed bent over like he was going to take off his shoes. Only he took off his legs! And then he pulled off his head!

I was getting pretty grossed out until I saw that his head was really a rubber mask, and his legs were really stilts.

I could hardly believe my eyes. Mr. Ed was really a little blue spaceman!

I screamed pretty loudly, which got Mr. Ed's attention.

"Please don't be afraid, earth being," he said. And for some reason, I wasn't.

"I have come to your planet in peace," Mr. Ed said. "I am here to study your people."

"To study us?" I asked.

Mr. Ed nodded. "You are my science project."

I laughed. Mr. Ed laughed, too. Then he said that earth beings are nicer in person than they are on television.

I decided to help him with his science project.
I explained that pencils are for writing, not
eating. I told him that the food in the cafeteria is
for eating—sort of.

Mr. Ed thanked me. Then he said he had
to go.

He let me watch his spaceship land. It was
really cool.

The next day Mrs. Barney was back. She told us she spent yesterday on a spaceship. She said she watched TV with little blue aliens.

I believed her, but no one else did. The
principal told her to take a nice, long vacation.
Guess who our substitute teacher was?

Mr. Ed! He came back for extra credit.

We learned a lot about each other every day. And I discovered that school can actually be a lot of fun.

Especially when your teacher is from outer space!